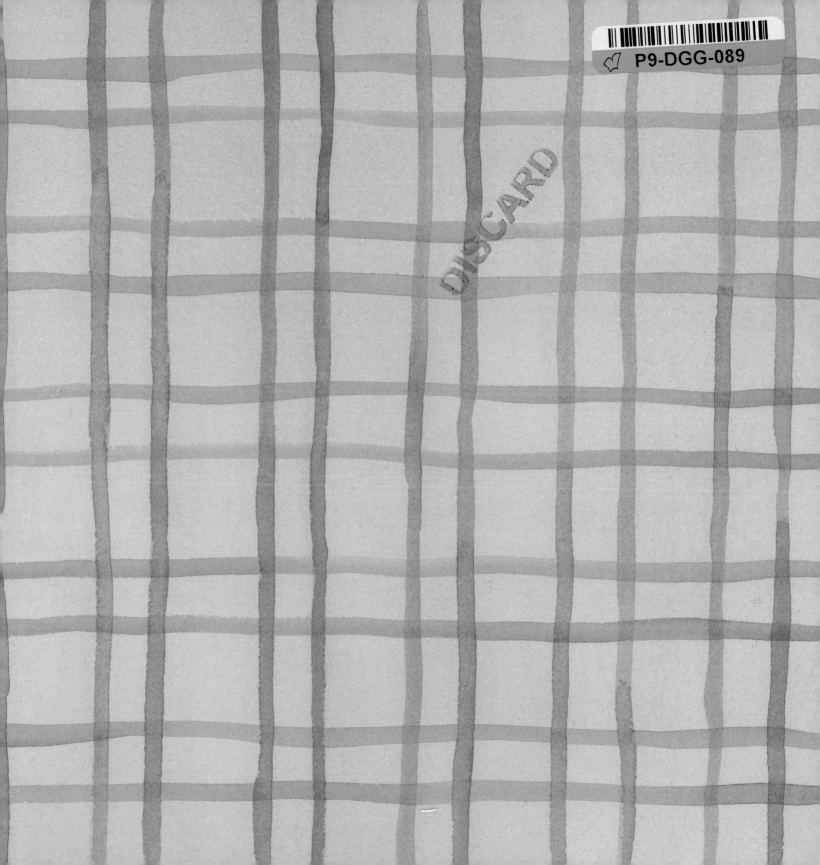

What a
BEAUTIFUL
MORNING

Arthur A. Levine

illustrated by KATIE KATH

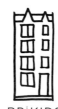

RP | KIDS
PHILADELPHIA • LONDON

Books published by Running Press are available at special discounts for bulk purchases in the United States
by corporations, institutions, and other organizations. For more information, please contact the
Special Markets Department at the Perseus Books Group, 2300 Chestnut Street, Suite 200,
Philadelphia, PA 19103, or call (800) 810-4145, ext. 5000, or e-mail special.markets@perseusbooks.com.

ISBN 978-0-7624-5906-3
Library of Congress Control Number: 2015960178

9 8 7 6 5 4 3 2 1
Digit on the right indicates the number of this printing

Designed by T.L. Bonaddio
Edited by Marlo Scrimizzi
Typography: Goudy and Dago

Published by Running Press Kids
An Imprint of Running Press Book Publishers
A Member of the Perseus Books Group
2300 Chestnut Street
Philadelphia, PA 19103–4371

Visit us on the web!
www.runningpress.com/rpkids

For my dad,
who felt that every morning was beautiful.
And for my mom
who keeps the song going.
—A. L.

To Ellen Ward,
for your strength, friendship, and loving kindness.
Also to my wonderful grandparents.
—K. K.

Summer days at Grandpa's house began
with a booming song . . .

. . . one with big round notes about
a beautiful morning, 'cause that's how
it felt to Grandpa and Noah. They
were already up to notice.

Grandma?

She didn't quite see it that way.

So Grandpa and Noah brought her a cup
of steaming coffee, which helped.
Then they took off down the road,
with the dog, singing . . .

raincoat and galoshes and
umbrella songs,
boats and beaches and sailors
come home songs,
bright breaking dawn through
the clouds songs . . .

Singing as long as the walk would last.

They even sang while Grandma made them cinnamon French toast.
Which sometimes led to slightly burned toast.

And nobody ever minded.

Then they'd talk about their plans for the rest of the day.

"What's on the docket?" Grandpa would ask.

And Noah always had dozens of docket ideas.

But this year, Grandpa forgot to ask what was on the docket almost every day.

One morning, he couldn't remember
how to cut his cinnamon French toast.

"Your fork is here, Grandpa,"
Noah said.

Then once, when Noah accidentally woke him from a nap, Grandpa looked scared and said, "Who are you? What are you doing here?"

Noah banged out the screen door and stood in the middle

of the lawn, breathing hard, a painful lump in his throat.

Grandma came outside after him and kneeled
down so she could look in his eyes.

She touched Noah's cheek, sighed, and said,
"Grandpa knows you. He just gets confused, that's all.
So we have to appreciate what he still has,
not focus on what he's lost."

Noah thought that was like trying
to feel good about the toys
you still had, when your favorite one
got left behind at the beach.

So Noah went ahead with his own docket . . .

He walked the dog.

He fed the birds.

He vroomed his trucks
up and over the spreading
swamp maple.

And he sat at the piano practicing "Doe, a Deer."
He sang the line about starting at the very beginning,
but then he played from the middle
(which he thought was an even better place to start).

Then suddenly, there was Grandpa, singing about a ray of golden sun!
And he sang the rest of the song, too, at the top of his lungs.

"Not bad, eh?" said Grandpa
when they finished.

"Not bad, Grandpa,"
said Noah.

At lunch, when Grandpa seemed lost, Noah sang Grandpa's favorite Tuna sandwich song, and sure enough, Grandpa's eyes got brighter and he joined right in. "Oh please, oh please, no celery for meeeee!"

Noah couldn't keep it up all day.

He was used to Grandpa starting the songs.

But Grandpa took a long nap and Grandma and Noah came up with a docket of their own . . .

They picked blueberries,

they got cream from
the market,

they collected recycled
treasures from the dump
to paint when they
got home.

And later, as they made meatballs together, Grandma said, "Hey, isn't there a Snoopy song about suppertime?"

Noah sang it bright and loud.

Grandpa looked surprised at first, but then . . .

He smiled just like he used to.
It was like the sun breaking
through clouds.

The next morning, Grandma got up
and made coffee for Grandpa.
"What's on the docket?" she asked Noah.

"Maybe a walk with Grandpa?" Noah said softly.

He wasn't sure.

But Grandma laid out Grandpa's walking clothes
and made sure Noah had a sweatshirt, too.

"Go ahead. Sing, bubbie," she said to Noah,
as he and Grandpa headed out the door
hand in hand.

And they took off down the road together,
planning to go for as long as the song would last.